WITH THANKS TO CLAIRE CARTEY
WHAT A WONDERFUL JOURNEY IT'S BEEN;
BOOKS, HUGS AND CAKE!

MONIKA AND LUKA —
NEVER TOO OLD TO HUG

www.huglessdouglas.co.uk

www.davidmelling.co.uk

Hugless Douglas and the Great Cake Bake

David Melling

Hodder Children's Books

Early one morning Douglas

was surprised to find a trail of footprints
running across his bed. They were sticky
and they tasted of honey!

'Who's been walking on **my** bed?' asked Douglas.

The honey-flavoured
footprints led all
the way to the
food cupboard.

'Where's my honey?' Douglas gasped. He looked at everything very carefully.

'I can't eat any of this without honey on top! And **I'M REALLY HUNGRY.**'

Douglas quickly changed and followed the honey trail outside.

'If only I could find a clue to help me,' he sighed.

Then Douglas twitched his nose.
'I know that smell...'

'Aaah, hello Douglas!' baaed the sheep.

'Why are you wearing my honey?' asked Douglas.

'We're collecting everything we need to bake
honey cakes,' said Flossie. 'Can you help?'

'Ooh yes,' said Douglas. 'I love baking.'

The sheep passed down BERRIES, NUTS, CARROTS AND HONEY.

Then Flossie made sure they all wore their proper outfits.

'And don't forget to wash your paws,' she said.

'Let's bake!'

Flossie shouted instructions from her
recipe book and they set to work.

'I've finished! Can I eat some now?' asked Douglas.
'Not yet, it needs baking first,' said Flossie. 'But
why not try these berries?'

'No thanks,' said Douglas, clutching his hungry
tummy. 'They haven't got honey on them. I'll wait.'

He watched the sheep put dollops
of the mixture onto baking trays
and into the oven.

By now, everyone was **very** hungry.
Douglas found a plate and joined the
back of a bad-tempered queue.
There was pushing and nudging.

Then someone threw a carrot…

B-DoINK!

PING! went the oven. The sheep froze.
'The cakes are ready!' said Flossie.

'Yay!' cried the sheep and they scrambled
towards the delicious smell.
'Save some for me!' called Douglas.

But the sheep didn't hear and
soon every single cake
had been eaten.

'What am I going to eat now?' said Douglas.
He looked at the carrots on the floor and sighed.

He bit into one. 'Oh,' he said, a little surprised. 'That's nice!' Douglas wasn't used to eating anything without honey on top.

He took a mouthful of berries. Even nicer!
And nuts... 'YuMMy!' he cried.

'Carrots, berries and nuts are ALMOST as good as honey,' said Douglas.

'But not quite. Nothing beats

HONEY
AND
HUGS!'

How to Decorate Cupcake Sheep...

1. Let your cakes cool.

3. Roll out the icing.

5. Add eyes, nose and ears.

Hugless Douglas and the Great Cake Bake
by David Melling

First published in 2016 by Hodder Children's Books

Text copyright © David Melling 2016
Illustration copyright © David Melling 2016

Hodder Children's Books
An imprint of
Hachette Children's Group
Part of Hodder & Stoughton
Carmelite House
50 Victoria Embankment
London EC4Y 0DZ

A catalogue record of this book is available from the British Library.

ISBN: 978 1 444 91988 2

10 9 8 7 6 5 4 3 2 1

Printed in China

An Hachette UK Company
www.hachette.co.uk